MEET THE CHARACTERS

BEN TENNYSON
TEN TIMES MORE TROUBLE THAN THE AVERAGE KID!

GWEN TENNYSON
RED-HEADED VOICE OF REASON TO HER COUSIN BEN

GRANDPA MAX
JUST A MILD-MANNERED GRANDFATHER – OR IS HE?...

VILGAX
ALIEN WARLORD WITH A REAL ATTITUDE PROBLEM

FOUR ARMS
PROOF THAT FOUR ARMS ARE BETTER THAN TWO

HEATBLAST
THIS ALIEN'S ON FIRE!

EGMONT
We bring stories to life

First published in Great Britain 2010 by Dean,
an imprint of Egmont UK Limited,
239 Kensington High Street, London W8 6SA
All Rights Reserved

ISBN 978 0 6035 6515 1
1 3 5 7 9 10 8 6 4 2
Printed and bound in Italy

BEN 10

PERMANENT RETIREMENT

BEN 10

PERMANENT RETIREMENT

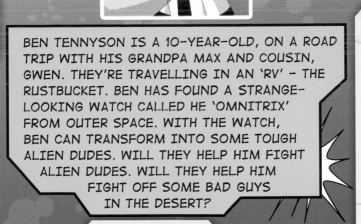

BEN TENNYSON IS A 10-YEAR-OLD, ON A ROAD TRIP WITH HIS GRANDPA MAX AND COUSIN, GWEN. THEY'RE TRAVELLING IN AN 'RV' – THE RUSTBUCKET. BEN HAS FOUND A STRANGE-LOOKING WATCH CALLED HE 'OMNITRIX' FROM OUTER SPACE. WITH THE WATCH, BEN CAN TRANSFORM INTO SOME TOUGH ALIEN DUDES. WILL THEY HELP HIM FIGHT ALIEN DUDES. WILL THEY HELP HIM FIGHT OFF SOME BAD GUYS IN THE DESERT?

BEN, GWEN AND GRANDPA MAX ARE DRIVING THROUGH THE DESERT. THEY STOP AT A SERVICE STATION FOR MAX TO TAKE OUT SOME CASH.

AS HE PUTS HIS CARD IN, MAX IS TOSSED ASIDE. A BAD-LOOKING DUDE HAS RIGGED UP A HOOK AND CHAIN TO THE CASH MACHINE. THE OTHER END OF THE CHAIN IS ATTACHED TO A TRUCK!

BEN RUSHES OVER AND PRESSES THE OMNITRIX ON HIS WRIST. HE TRANSFORMS INTO UPGRADE! THE GOOD GUY ALIEN THEN MERGES INTO THE TRUCK AND TAKES CONTROL OF IT!

YOUR CASH REQUEST HAS BEEN DENIED!

UPGRADE GRABS THE CHAIN AND FLOORS THE BAD GUYS WITH IT. JOB DONE – THEY'RE POWERLESS AGAINST THIS SUPERHERO!

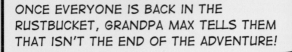

ONCE EVERYONE IS BACK IN THE RUSTBUCKET, GRANDPA MAX TELLS THEM THAT ISN'T THE END OF THE ADVENTURE!

WE'RE OFF TO SEE YOUR AUNT VERA FOR THE WEEKEND.

BORING OLD AUNT VERA! OH MAN, THIS SUMMER WAS SUPPOSED TO BE ABOUT FUN!

"I LIKE AUNT VERA," SAYS GWEN.

DUH, THAT'S BECAUSE YOU ACT LIKE YOU'RE A HUNDRED YEARS OLD!

AUNT VERA LIVES IN A RETIREMENT VILLAGE, BUT IT'S NOT QUITE WHAT BEN EXPECTS. GLANCING OUT THE WINDOW, BEN SEES AN OLD MAN ON THE ROOF OF HIS HOUSE, FIXING A SATELLITE DISH. SUDDENLY HE SLIPS, AND IS ABOUT TO PLUMMET TO THE GROUND WHEN HE DOES A MID-AIR FLIP AND LANDS ON HIS FEET!

WHEN THEY ARRIVE AT VERA'S HOUSE, BEN SPOTS HER OLD NEIGHBOUR, MARTY, LOOKING OUT OF HIS WINDOW. THE MAN GROWLS, CRACKS AND TWISTS HIS NECK, AND SHUTS HIS BLINDS. *WEIRD!*

JUST WATCH YOUR CHEEKS, VERA'S A PINCHER!

GRANDPA MAX'S WARNING COMES TOO LATE AS AUNT VERA PINCHES BEN AND GWEN'S CHEEKS AND GIVES THEM ALL A BIG HUG! "SHEESH", THINKS BEN.

EVEN VERA'S CANDY ISN'T NORMAL! WHAT SHOULD TASTE SWEET TURNS OUT TO BE LUMPS OF COFFEE ...
COFFEE!
"COFFEE! AS A CANDY? IS THIS SOME KIND OF JOKE? I NEED TO USE THE BATHROOM," GASPS BEN.
"IT'S THE ATTACK OF THE OLD PEOPLE," THINKS BEN. "I GOTTA GET OUTTA HERE."
BEN DECIDES IT'S TIME TO GO GHOSTFREAK!

THERE HAS TO BE SOMETHING FUN TO DO AROUND HERE.

GHOSTFREAK DRIFTS OUTSIDE. ACROSS THE STREET AN OLD WOMAN IS TRYING TO SWAT A FLY IN HER HOUSE. MISSING A COUPLE OF SWATS, SHE HAS A BETTER IDEA. SHE RUNS UP ONE OF THE WALLS, GRABS THE FLY, FLIPS IN THE AIR AND LANDS ON HER FEET. THEN SHE EATS IT!

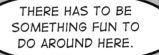

NO WAY! NINJA OLD PEOPLE!

BACK ON THE STREET ...

NEIGHBOUR MARTY SPEEDS BY IN A GOLF BUGGY. IN THE BACK THERE'S A ROLLED-UP CARPET. MARTY STOPS NEAR A LARGE RUBBISH SKIP SURROUNDED BY A GATE. CARRYING THE CARPET, MARTY SLITHERS THROUGH THE GATE WITHOUT OPENING IT!

"THIS PLACE JUST KEEPS GETTING WEIRDER BY THE MINUTE," THINKS GHOSTFREAK.

GHOSTFREAK FOLLOWS MARTY.

MARTY OPENS UP A TRAP DOOR BENEATH THE SKIP. SUDDENLY THE OMNITRIX STARTS TO *BLEEP* ... AND BEN IS BACK!

MARTY DROPS THE CARPET AND LUNGES AT BEN. BUT BEN WRIGGLES FREE AND RUNS TOWARDS THE GOLF BUGGY. MARTY CHASES AFTER HIM!

WHAT KIND OF VITAMINS ARE THESE FREAKY OLD PEOPLE TAKING?

BEN SPEEDS OFF, BUT MARTY'S ARMS HAVE STRETCHED LIKE ELASTIC! MARTY PULLS HIMSELF ON TO THE BUGGY, MAKING BEN LOSE CONTROL AND CRASH INTO A WATER SPRINKLER. MARTY'S STRETCHY ARMS SUDDENLY SHOOT BACK INTO HIS BODY, AND HE DISAPPEARS ...

BEN RACES THROUGH AUNT VERA'S FRONT DOOR.

GRANDPA! GWEN!

"SHHHH! AUNT VERA'S IN BED," WHISPERS MAX.

THIS PLACE IS WAY CREEPY! FIRST THIS OLD LADY RUNS UP A WALL. THEN MARTY, THAT WEIRD NEIGHBOUR HAS THESE LONG STICKY ARMS AND THIS BODY THAT OOZED RIGHT THROUGH A GATE ...

OK, SOUNDS LIKE WE SHOULD DO SOME INVESTIGATING ...

BEN, GWEN AND GRANDPA MAX CREEP INTO MARTY'S HOUSE. THEY TAKE A GOOD LOOK AROUND, BUT EVERYTHING LOOKS PRETTY NORMAL. "LET'S CHECK THINGS OUT AGAIN IN THE MORNING," SAYS MAX.

BUT THAT NIGHT, IN AUNT VERA'S BEDROOM, A GLOB OF SOMETHING *STRANGE* CRAWLS ALONG THE FLOOR TOWARDS HER BED. IT SLITHERS ON TO VERA, AND CUPS ITS HAND OVER HER MOUTH SO SHE CANNOT SCREAM ...

BEN AND GWEN HEAD FOR THE RUBBISH SKIP AND THE TRAP DOOR, WHERE MARTY WAS THE NIGHT BEFORE.

THEY PASS TWO OLD WOMEN PLAYING A GAME OF SHUFFLEBOARD. THE WOMEN LOOK UP AND HISS. THEY PICK UP THEIR STICKS AND START BATTING THE HARD ROUND SHUFFLEBOARD PLATES AT BEN AND GWEN! THEY *ZIP* THROUGH THE AIR LIKE MISSILES.

DUCK!

RUN!

BEN AND GWEN DIVE OUT OF THE WAY JUST (AND ONLY JUST) IN TIME! THEY SPRINT ROUND A CORNER AND FIND THEMSELVES CLOSE TO THE RUBBISH SKIP. GRANDPA MAX HEADS TOWARDS THEM.

BEN AND GWEN REACH THE RUBBISH SKIP. "TIME TO GO WILDMUTT," BEN DECIDES.
WILDMUTT PUSHES THE RUBBISH SKIP TO ONE SIDE AND OPENS THE TRAP DOOR UNDERNEATH. GWEN LEAPS ON TO WILDMUTT'S BACK AND THEY DROP THROUGH THE TRAP DOOR, AND FALL INTO THE DARKNESS ...
HEY, WILDMUTT, DOES THE EXPRESSION 'LOOK BEFORE YOU LEAP' MEAN ANYTHING TO YOU?
THE OLD FOLKS SLITHER DOWN AFTER THEM ...

WILDMUTT AND GWEN RACE ALONG DARK UNDERGROUND TUNNELS. GRANDPA MAX CATCHES UP WITH THEM BUT WILDMUTT PINS HIM DOWN.
"YOU WOULDN'T WANT TO HURT OLD GRANDPA MAX, NOW WOULD YA?" BEGS MAX.
SUDDENLY, GRANDPA MAX WINGS AT WILDMUTT AND SENDS HIM LYING AGAINST THE TUNNEL WALL!
"HEY, SHORT, DUMB AND HAIRY! RULE ONE, HE'S NOT GRANDPA! HE'S AN ALIEN FREAK. AND RULE TWO ... WE KICK ALIEN BUTT!" SAYS GWEN.
WHOA!
WILDMUTT KNOCKS GRANDPA MAX DOWN, THEN STOPS AND SNIFFS THE AIR. HE'S PICKED UP A SCENT! WILDMUTT AND GWEN BOLT DOWN A SIDE TUNNEL.
SLOW DOWN! YOU DON'T COME WITH SEATBELTS, REMEMBER?

UH-OH! THE OMNITRIX STARTS TO BLEEP. WILDMUTT POWERS DOWN BACK INTO BEN.

BEEP!

BEN AND GWEN DISCOVER THAT THE TUNNEL IS FILLED WITH DOZENS OF PODS CONTAINING SLUMBERING OLD PEOPLE!

IT'S LIKE EVERYONE IN THE RETIREMENT VILLAGE HAS BEEN PODDED UP.

ONE OF THE PODS HAS GRANDPA MAX INSIDE!

BEN RIPS IT OPEN AND OUT FALLS A GROGGY GRANDPA MAX. IT'S AS IF HE'S JUST WOKEN UP FROM A DEEP SLEEP.

I WAS OUT FOR A WALK AND THEN ... I CAN'T REMEMBER WHAT HAPPENED NEXT.

WANDERING AROUND, GWEN TOUCHES A STRANGE WALL. IT OPENS UP TO REVEAL THE ENTRANCE TO A **SPACESHIP!** EVERYONE HAS FORGOTTEN ABOUT THE MENACING OLD FOLKS. SUDDENLY THEY SURROUND BEN, GWEN AND GRANDPA MAX. INSIDE THE UNDERGROUND SPACESHIP ARE MORE PODS, AND IN ONE OF THEM IS AUNT VERA!

"TIME TO GO HEATBLAST!" SAYS BEN.

YOU GUYS REALLY BURN ME UP, NOW I'M GOING TO RETURN THE FAVOUR!

SOME OF THE LIMAX OLD FOLKS GO FOR HEATBLAST. HE THROWS MASSIVE BLASTS OF FIRE AT THEM. SUDDENLY, ALL THE LIMAXES COME TOGETHER TO FORM ONE HUGE ALIEN!

WHATEVER YOU ARE, YOU JUST MADE A **TERRIBLE** MISTAKE. WE LIMAXES LIVE FOR THE HEAT! WHY DO YOU THINK WE CAME TO THE DESERT IN THE SUMMER?

THE LIMAX GRABS HEATBLAST AND TOSSES HIM THROUGH THE AIR. HE CRASHES AGAINST A WALL BUT GETS RIGHT BACK UP AGAIN.

WITH ALL THE FIGHTING, GWEN'S BACKPACK IS KNOCKED, AND HER WATER GUN FALLS OUT. SOME OTHER LIMAXES SEE THAT THE GUN IS FULL OF WATER AND THEY BACK AWAY. GWEN GRABS THE GUN AND FIRES AT THE LIMAXES. THEY DISSOLVE!

THEY *HATE* WATER! AUNT VERA WHEN SHE WAS IN THE KITCHEN ...

... AND MARTY WHEN I WAS ON THE GOLF BUGGY!

HEATBLAST SPOTS SOME WATER PIPES ON THE CEILING. HE SHOOTS A BLAST OF FIRE AT THE PIPES AND THEY MELT, POURING WATER OVER THE HUGE LIMAX. WITH A FINAL GASP, THE GIANT LIMAX DISSOLVES!

BACK ON THE SPACESHIP, GWEN AND GRANDPA MAX ARE CARRYING THE LAST OF THE PODS AWAY, INCLUDING AUNT VERA'S. ONE LAST LIMAX SLITHERS ON BOARD. THERE'S A HUGE ROAR, AND GWEN AND GRANDPA MAX MAKE IT OUT OF THE SPACESHIP JUST IN TIME AS A DOOR CLOSES BEHIND THEM ...

WHOOSH!

THE SPACESHIP BLASTS UP THROUGH THE GROUND, LEAVING A HUGE CRATER AS IT RISES INTO THE AIR! HEATBLAST, GWEN AND MAX FIND THEMSELVES IN THE DESERT, SURROUNDED BY ALL THE PODS.

WE SHOULD PUT THEM ALL BACK IN THEIR HOMES SO THEY THINK THEY NEVER LEFT.

GIMME A FEW MINUTES, I'LL SEE IF XLR8 CAN HELP OUT.